Enid Blyton's
TELL-A-STORY BOOK

Sneezing Powder
and other stories

The Silver Trails

THERE was once a snail who was very friendly with the elf who lived under the pansies. Every night the snail used to go and see his friend, and they played together.

Little Hands, the elf, loved to see how the snail could pop his eyes in and out of his horns. It always seemed queer to her that he should have eyes at the tops of his horns, and queerer still that he could pull them in and out.

She liked riding on his back too, though he was a very slow horse, but she thought it was clever of him to take his house with him wherever he went. After all, anyone would be slow if he had to carry his own house everywhere!

One night when the snail went to see Little Hands, she was gone. The pansies were broken and torn. What could have happened?

A nearby beetle told the snail the whole story. "You know that goblin who lives in a hole in the wall up there?" he said. "Well, he came and captured poor Little Hands. She screamed and struggled, but it wasn't any use. She had to go with him. Isn't it a pity?"

"Oh dear! I must go and rescue her," said the snail at once, and set off on his slow way to the wall. It was a dry night, and the snail had to try to keep his body slimy so that he could slide along easily. The slime made a pretty silvery trail behind him as he went.

Soon he came to the wall. He knew the hole where the goblin lived. He heard someone crying there, and he guessed it was Little Hands. He crawled near the hole.

"Little Hands, come out!" he whispered. "Is the goblin asleep? Come out, and I will block up the hole with my shell so that he can't follow you."

Little Hands ran out at once, and the snail

crawled into the hole and blocked it up with his stout shell. The goblin awoke when he heard the elf running away, and he ran after her. But what was this blocking up his door? A snail! How dare he?

The goblin pushed and shoved, but it was no use at all. He couldn't move the snail. He was a prisoner in his own hole!

He shouted and kicked and fetched a little hammer to try to break the snail's shell. But he couldn't. So in the end he had to go back to bed.

"I know you'll crawl off as soon as I'm asleep, Snail," he said, "but I shall know where you go because you always leave a silvery trail behind you. I shall see it tomorrow morning, and follow it to your hiding-place. Then I will fetch the hungry thrush and he will break your shell and eat you."

The snail did not answer. But as soon as he heard the goblin snoring, he crawled quietly away. He went down the wall, leaving his tell-tale trail behind him. Then he found some of his snail friends and spoke to them.

"Please help me," he said. "The goblin is going to follow my trail. Will you all crawl to and fro and round about me, so that my trail and yours are all muddled up? Oh, thank you!"

When morning came the snail-trails were so mixed and tangled that no one, not even the goblin, could possibly follow the right one! The snail is safe in my garden now, and I have a feeling that Little Hands is somewhere about too. I really must look.

Mrs. Tap-Tap-Tap

NOBODY knew what the little old lady's real name was. Everyone called her Mrs. Tap-Tap-Tap, because she tapped with her stick as she walked.

You see, she was blind, and she couldn't see, so she had to take a stick with her wherever she went, to tap along the pavement to find the kerb.

She was a nice cheery old lady, and she often went out for walks by herself, but she could never cross the road unless somebody helped her, because she couldn't see if any motors were coming.

The children were very good to her. As soon as any boy or girl saw Mrs. Tap-Tap-Tap waiting at the kerb to cross the road, one of them would go up to her and take her arm. Then, as soon as the road was clear, they would take her safely across to the other side.

"Thank you, my dear," Mrs. Tap-Tap-Tap would say, and off she would go on her way again, tap-tap-tapping with her stick.

One of the children who helped Mrs. Tap-Tap-

Tap a great deal was Johnny Watson. He always met her as he went home from afternoon school, and often she waited for him to help her across the road.

"Hallo, Johnny!" she would say, as he came running up behind her. "I always know the sound of your feet."

"Hallo, Mrs. Tap-Tap-Tap!" Johnny would say. "Let me help you across the road. Wait a moment—there's a car. Now it's gone. We are safe."

This happened nearly every afternoon, and Johnny liked Mrs. Tap-Tap-Tap very much, because she always had a joke for him.

Now, one November afternoon, a thick fog came down, and when Johnny came out from school he could hardly see the school gates. At first he thought it was fun. Then he didn't—because he found that everywhere looked so very different, and he began to feel that he didn't know the way home.

"It's this way," he said to himself, as he felt along the railings near by. "I shall come to a corner here."

But he didn't. There didn't seem to be a corner anywhere. He went back again, and tried to find the school gates so that he could start off home again. But he couldn't find the gates!

"This horrid fog makes everything as dark as night," said Johnny, trying not to feel frightened. "Oh dear—wherever am I? I really don't know. I am quite lost."

He stood where he was for a little while, hoping that somebody would come along and he could ask the way. But nobody came. Everyone was safe at home.

Johnny set off again, trying to read the names of the houses, so that he might know where he was. But it was too foggy even to do that.

At last he stood still again, thinking that he must be going even farther away from home instead of getting nearer. And then he heard someone coming!

Tap-Tap-Tap! Tap-Tap-Tap! That was the noise he heard.

"Goodness! It must be Mrs. Tap-Tap-Tap's stick!" said Johnny. "Fancy her being out on a dreadful day like this! I hope she isn't lost too."

Presently Mrs. Tap-Tap-Tap came right by Johnny. He put out his hand and stopped her.

"Mrs. Tap-Tap-Tap, are you lost, too?" he asked.

"Lost?" said the old lady in surprise. "Of course not! Why should I be?"

"Well, it's as dark as night today, with this thick fog," said Johnny.

"Little boy, it is always as dark as night to me," said Mrs. Tap-Tap-Tap. "Blind people are always in the dark, you know—so what's a fog to me? I know my way as well in a fog as I do in the sunlight."

"Do you really?" said Johnny, most surprised. "I never thought of that."

"Ah, Johnny, you may be able to get home all

right in the daylight, but I'm cleverer than you in a fog," chuckled Mrs. Tap-Tap-Tap. "It seems to me, Johnny, that *I* shall have to help *you* today! Well, that will be a pleasant change! Come along with me. My house is just near here. We'll have a cup of tea together, and then *I* will take *you* home."

Johnny slipped his hand under the old lady's arm and went along with her. She knew her way well. She tap-tapped with her stick, turned the right corners, and knew just which way to go. At last she came to a little house. She took the key from her pocket and opened the door. In they went.

A little round fat maid came running up the hall. "I'm glad to see you safe, Mam!" she cried.

"Safe as can be!" said the old lady. "Now, Janet, bring us tea and toast and some of my best short-bread. We have a visitor today—somebody who has helped me a lot at one time and another."

Soon Johnny and Mrs. Tap-Tap-Tap were sitting down and eating a delicious tea. Then Mrs. Tap-Tap-Tap put on her hat again and set off down the street with Johnny. It was still very foggy—but the old lady didn't mind about that. No—*she* could see as well in the dark as in the light!

It wasn't long before they came to Johnny's home. Johnny's mother was so glad to see him. She hadn't worried about him really, because she had thought he was staying to tea at school as it was so foggy. She thanked Mrs. Tap-Tap-Tap very kindly for bringing Johnny home safely.

"Oh, your Johnny has often done me a good turn," said the old lady, smiling. "Now it's my turn to do him a good turn. Good-bye, Johnny! You'll see me across the road safely tomorrow, if it's fine, won't you?"

"Of course I will!" said Johnny. "I'll be your eyes on a sunny day—and you can be mine on a foggy one!"

Twinkle's Fur Coat

THERE was once an elf who wanted a fur coat. Her friend, Ripple the Pixie, had one, and so had old Goody Tiptap over the road.

"I want one, too," sighed Twinkle the Elf. "A fur coat looks so nice, and keeps people so warm. Ripple, did your fur coat cost very much money to buy?"

"Yes, very, very much," said Ripple. "It took a whole year's savings."

"Goody Tiptap, was *your* fur coat expensive to buy?" asked Twinkle, as Goody came by.

"It belonged to my mother," said Goody Tiptap. "Her brother was a hunter, and he brought home the skins for a coat. I do not know if it would be dear to buy."

Twinkle counted out her money. She had two five pence pieces, a ten pence, and a fifty pence piece. That was all.

"Certainly not enough to buy a fur coat," thought Twinkle sadly.

She put the money back into her money-box. "I shan't think any more about a fur coat," she said. "I shall go and call on my Aunt Tabitha, and take her some flowers out of my garden—that is, if I can find any! The poor things are dying because we haven't had any rain for so long."

She found some flowers and made them into a nice bunch, and set off to her Aunt Tabitha's. On the way there she heard a good deal of squeaking, and she crept through the grass to see what it was all about. She peeped from behind a buttercup—and in a circle of grass she saw twelve furry caterpillars holding a meeting.

"Good gracious!" said Twinkle in surprise. "I never saw caterpillars holding a meeting before. I wonder what it's all about."

She went to see. The caterpillars turned to her as she spoke.

"Whatever's the matter?" asked Twinkle.

"Matter enough!" said the largest furry caterpillar. "Do you know, all our food-plants are dying for want of rain, and we haven't enough to eat!"

"Really!" said Twinkle, surprised. "Well, what are you going to do?"

"We don't know," said the caterpillars sadly. "We could go and find some other place where the plants are better perhaps—but we don't know which way to go."

"What sort of plants do you want?" asked Twinkle.

"Well, we like plantains and nettles—and lettuce is a big treat, though we hardly ever get it," said the biggest caterpillar, waving his black head at Twinkle.

"Now listen," said Twinkle. "I'm going for a walk to my Aunt Tabitha's. On the way I will see if I can find any good food-plants for you to eat. Maybe I can find some in a ditch, where it is damp. I will tell you if I do, and show you the way there."

"Oh, thank you," said the big caterpillar. "You see, it is nearly time for us to change into a chrysalis and sleep, but we do need a good meal first."

Twinkle set off. All the way to her aunt's she kept a look-out for some nice juicy green plants for the hungry caterpillars—but alas! everything looked dry and dead. No rain had fallen for three weeks, and the plants were dying.

"Isn't it dreadful!" thought Twinkle, as she set off back home again. Her aunt was out, so Twinkle had just popped into the kitchen and put her flowers in water on the table. "Isn't it dreadful! No food for the poor caterpillars! All the plantains are dead and dry, and the nettles are grey instead of green! How everything does want rain."

She came back to the caterpillars. She looked at them sadly and shook her head.

"It's sad," she said, "but everywhere is the same. There isn't a thing for you to eat!"

"Then we shall die," said the biggest caterpillar. "And oh, what a pity it is, because after one more good feed we should each be ready to turn into a chrysalis, and sleep until we had changed into a beautiful tiger moth!"

"Oh, do you turn into those lovely red-and-black

17

tiger moths?" cried Twinkle in excitement. "The Fairy Queen has those to ride on when she goes for a moonlight flight! I've seen her— and once she let *me* ride on one of her tiger moths, and it was lovely! It fluttered its big coloured wings, and off we went into the air."

"Well, I'm afraid the Queen will not have many tiger moths to ride this year," said the big caterpillar. "If only we could get something green and juicy to eat—but it's no use if you say that everything is dried up."

"Listen!" said Twinkle suddenly. "I will tell you what to do. I have a lettuce-bed, and you shall come with me and eat some of my lettuces. Then you will each be able to turn into a chrysalis, and the Queen will have her tiger moths to ride on."

"Oh, thank you, Twinkle!" squeaked all the caterpillars. Then, with Twinkle leading the way, they all followed her in a long, furry line, their dark brown bodies going up and down, up and down, as they walked over the field.

What a feast those caterpillars had in Twinkle's lettuces! Twinkle really was surprised to see how much they could eat. Their jaws opened and shut as they chewed the green lettuce leaves, and soon there were very, very few lettuces left. Twinkle was rather sad. She hadn't thought that caterpillars could eat so much!

The next day the big caterpillar spoke to her. "Thank you!" he said. "Thank you! Now we shall not eat any more. The time has come for each of us to turn into a chrysalis."

"May I watch you?" asked Twinkle. "It always seems such strange and powerful magic to me when a caterpillar changes into a chrysalis, and then comes out of the chrysalis as a moth or a butterfly! How does your caterpillar body change into a moth's body with lovely big wings, Caterpillar?"

"We don't know," said the furry caterpillar. "It is a strange spell, and we don't understand it. Of course you can watch us, little elf. You have been very kind to us. Now are you ready, caterpillars? Then first of all take off your furry skins! You will not want those in the chrysalis!"

So every caterpillar shed its furry coat—and there were all the little furs lying on the ground! The elf suddenly gave a cry of delight, and shouted to the caterpillars:

"Don't you want your furry skins any more? Can I have them, please?"

"Of course," said the big caterpillar. "If you don't have them, I expect the mice will come along and eat them, or the beetles. Whatever do you want them for?"

"Ah, you will see when you change into moths and come creeping out of your chrysalises," said Twinkle.

She collected all the furry skins and ran off to the house with them. She washed them well. She hung them on the line to dry. She took her needle and

19

thimble and thread, and she began to sew.

How she sewed! She sewed all those little furry caterpillar skins together, and made a beautiful fur coat from them! You should have seen it! It fitted her beautifully, and was so warm and cosy.

When she had finished the coat, she shook it out and then went to see what had happened to the

caterpillars. They were all fast asleep in tight black chrysalis cases! Twinkle touched one—and it wriggled.

"They are alive, but sleeping," said the elf. "How strange that they are growing into moths whilst they sleep! I will wait until they awake—and then I will show them my fur coat."

Weeks later the caterpillars awoke, each in his hard little chrysalis case—but they were no longer caterpillars! They had changed magically into magnificent moths—tiger moths with bright red, cream, and black wings, beautiful to see!

Twinkle watched each moth make a hole in its case and creep out. Their wings were damp and crumpled—but in an hour or two each moth had dried its lovely wings, and was fluttering them in the air.

"Oh, do you remember me?" cried the elf, dancing up to them. "You knew me when you were furry caterpillars. You gave me your furry skins when you took them off for the last time! Look at the lovely fur coat I made from your skins!"

The bright moths looked at her, and waved their feelers about.

"Yes, we remember you," said the biggest moth. "You were the elf who helped us—and we are glad we gave you our skins to make you a fur coat. You deserve it! We will give you a ride too, any night you want one. You are a kind little thing."

They spread their wings and flew off to the Queen; but sometimes, when the Queen can spare one of her moths, he flies back to Twinkle and gives her a ride through the moonlit wood. She puts on her warm fur coat then, and looks perfectly sweet.

Wasn't it a cheap fur coat? It only cost a few lettuces and a bit of kindness!

Green-Caps

GREEN-CAPS the goblin set up his little shop in the middle of the poppies. He loved their bright red flowers, and they in turn liked the merry little goblin who worked so hard in his tiny shop.

You can guess what Green-caps' work was. He made green hats for the little folk—nicely fitting little caps into which they could stick any coloured feather they liked. One by one the pixies, the brownies, the elves, and the goblins came to him for a hat. He made them all neatly, and his stitches were so tiny that they could hardly be seen.

The poppies watched him sewing busily each day. They nodded their red heads and spoke together.

"We would like green caps too."

"But what would be the sense of that?" asked Green-caps in surprise. "You could not wear my small green caps on your big red heads."

"We would like green caps for our *buds*," said the poppies, nodding in the wind. "You know, Goblin, when we are in bud, sometimes the winds are cold and they make us shiver. If we could wear green caps that fitted us well, we would be warm and cosy. We need not open our petals until the sun is really hot. The caps would keep us closed."

"But when you opened your pretty petals, the caps would look silly," said the goblin.

"We would throw them down to the ground as soon as we opened," said the poppies. "We shouldn't need them then. You could use them again, couldn't you, Green-caps?"

"Well—that's an idea," said the goblin. "I will make you some little caps for your buds and see if they will be of any use."

So Green-caps got busy and measured the buds for caps. He made some dear little round ones in green that fitted the buds tightly. He put one on each tiny bud.

"Now," he said to them, "when you feel that the sun is warm and you want to open and shake out your crumpled petals to dry, push hard at the cap— and it will split down the seams and fall off to the ground. Then I will come along and collect the pieces to make new caps."

The buds loved their green caps. They wore them as long as they needed warmth and protection— then they pushed them off so hard that they burst the seams—and the cap fell to the ground in pieces. Then the poppy shook out its silky red petals, and danced in the sun.

Green-caps came along, picked up the fallen pieces of cap, took them home and sewed them neatly together again into another cap for a small bud.

Soon many little folk came to see the green caps he made for the poppies, because, as you can guess, the poppies talked about them to everyone. That meant a great deal more business for the goblin— and soon he was so busy that he had to send for more workers to help him. He still works among the poppies, as busy as can be, though he pops down a rabbit-hole if you come near.

But though he hides himself, he can't hide the green caps he makes for the poppies! Go and have a look at them in the summer-time. You will find some poppies wearing them neatly, others just pushing them off, and still others with no caps at all, for they have burst the seams that Green-caps sewed—and the pieces are lying on the ground. If there are none on the ground you will know why— Green-caps has been there before you and picked them all up!

The Magic Duster

HEYHO the goblin had made a Magic Duster. My word, he was proud of it too! Just a flick with that duster would make anything shine and glitter as brightly as the sun!

"I shall make some money out of this!" said Heyho to himself. "I'll go round and offer to polish when people are doing their spring-cleaning. They will find my magic duster very useful!"

So in the spring he went around to the pixies, elves, brownies, and gnomes, and offered the use of his wonderful duster.

"Just a flick and all your silver will gleam like the river!" he said. "Just a rub and your old paint will shine like new! Just a touch and your floors will be slippery enough to dance on all night long!"

Well, everyone borrowed that duster, you may be sure! Gobo the gnome borrowed it for his silver bowls and cups, the ones he had won for being the fastest runner in the village. Twinkle the elf borrowed it for her beautiful old furniture, and after a flick and a rub all her dark brown chairs and tables and stools glowed and shone in a marvellous manner.

"It certainly saves a lot of work," said Twinkle. "It would have taken me weeks to polish all my furniture properly."

Henny-Penny borrowed it to polish her chicks' beaks, and all the blackbirds did the same. Everybody had to pay Heyho a ten pence piece, so he soon became very rich.

And then the Queen heard of the magic duster and she sent for Heyho. He was as proud as could be when he got the message, and off he went to the palace.

Well, the Queen wanted a good deal done, and she hoped that the magic duster could do it.

"I want my beautiful old glasses and jugs polished," she said. "And I want all the windows done. And you might do the paint whilst you are here, and all the silver and gold plate, too."

So Heyho was quite busy for a day, for although he just had to flick here and there, there were a good many flicks to get through! Soon all the windows, the glasses, the silver, and the gold, and the paint gleamed and shone and glittered and glowed. Everybody admired Heyho's work, and he began to get very vain and conceited.

"This is nothing to what I *can* do!" he said. "I'll do a few things that the Queen hasn't asked for, and you'll see how marvellous my duster is!"

"No, you mustn't do anything you have not been told to do," said the butler at once. Heyho grinned cheekily at him. He meant to do just exactly what he pleased!

Well, that night, when everyone was in bed, he went to the golden thrones of the King and Queen

27

and rubbed them lightly with his magic duster. How they shone! How they glittered! But, dear me, how slippery they were!

He flicked his duster over the beautiful wooden floors, and they too glowed. They were very slippery with the magic, and Heyho at once fell down three times before he managed to get into the hall.

And then, just for fun, he did a very naughty thing. He flicked his duster over all the boots and shoes lying in the kitchen for the kitchen-maid to clean the next morning! He meant to shine up the tops of the boots and shoes, but he knew quite well that his duster would send its magic shine on to the bottoms of the shoes as well; and, dear me, nobody likes slippery shoes to walk on!

Then he went to bed, wondering what everyone would say the next day.

Things happened quickly the next morning. The two footmen who carried coal to make the fires in the Queen's breakfast-room had to walk along the slippery floor. Down they went, and all the coal flew into every corner. The King and Queen woke up in a fright, and the King put on his dressing-gown and went to see what was the matter.

Of course, as soon as he put his feet on the slippery stairs they flew from under him, and he went down with a dreadful bump!

How he roared! And plenty of other people roared too, when they found that they couldn't walk on the gleaming, slippery floors! Down went breakfast-trays, down went brushes and brooms and pans, crash—thud—bang!

The butler ordered carpets to be nailed on to the floors, but, good gracious me, things didn't seem very much better, for as soon as anyone wore the boots or shoes that Heyho had rubbed with his magic duster, down they went, whether they walked on carpet or wooden floor! They simply could not stand on their slippery soles.

The butler complained to the King and Queen. "Someone's been playing a bad joke," he said. "And I think I know who it is!"

"I think I do too," said the King grimly. "Call everyone, and I and the Queen will find the joker and punish him."

So in a little while all the servants stood in the great hall, and the King and Queen walked to their golden thrones.

But they couldn't sit on them! Heyho had made them so slippery with his magic duster that as soon as the King and the Queen sat on the polished seats they slid off them, and sat on the ground!

So they had to stand, and the King's frown was like a black thunder-cloud. It made Heyho tremble when he was brought before all the servants and before their Majesties too!

"Take hold of this silly goblin and throw him up into the moon," commanded the King. "I'm tired of him!"

Heyho hadn't time to squeal or to beg for mercy. Two strong footmen took hold of him, swung him in front of the open window two or three times, and then let go! Up he went in the air, up and up and up! But he didn't quite reach the moon, for it happened to be rather far away that day. So he fell back to earth again, and dropped into a hawthorn hedge which pricked him hard, but held him fast so that he wasn't hurt much.

All round him was a golden buttercup-field, and a little elf was patiently polishing the cups as they opened. It was a long, long job. Heyho watched for a moment. Then he took out his magic duster and flung it to the elf.

"Take it!" he said. "It's got me into dreadful trouble, and I'd better not use it any more. But you're welcome to it. Good-bye, I'm off to the land of Never-Never, where I hope I'll never-never get into trouble again!"

So off he went—and he's never-never been heard of since. But the elf uses that duster every summer. She just flicks it round a buttercup-field, and her work is done! Every buttercup shines as if it had been well polished and gleams like gold. Pick one and look into it. Isn't it beautifully polished?

Nobody Came to Tea

THERE was once a lonely hare. He hadn't any friends, and he wanted some.

He talked to the scarecrow in the field, and the scarecrow gave him some advice.

"Ask people to tea. They like that. That is what children do. Give a party sometime, and ask all the creatures to come."

It was summer-time when the scarecrow told the hare this. The hare felt excited. "It will take me a long time to get things for the party," he said. "I will ask everyone for the last week in October. Then I shall have plenty of time to collect food for my guests."

He asked the little dormouse, who was delighted. He asked the prickly hedgehog, and he was very pleased. He asked both the frog and the toad, and as they were cousins they said they would come together.

"That's four," said the hare. "Now, who's next to be asked? Oh yes—I'll ask the lizard and the snake, and I'll ask the little black bat too. He will enjoy a party. I must try to get some beetles for him."

So he asked them all, and they said yes, they would all come to tea with him and be friends.

"Seven guests," the hare told the scarecrow. "It's a *real* party, isn't it?"

Well, the day of the party came. The hare had collected food for every one of his guests, and he set it all out in his field.

Then he waited for his visitors to come. But nobody came to tea. Nobody at all. The dormouse didn't turn up, and neither did the hedgehog. The frog and toad were not to be seen. The lizard didn't come frisking along, and no gliding, silent snake came to tea. Even the little black bat was missing too.

The hare was sad. "Nobody likes me," he said. "Nobody has come to tea. They said they would—but they were making fun of me. They didn't mean to come."

"What's the matter," said the rabbit, who was passing by. The hare told him. The rabbit laughed loudly.

"Silly hare! The dormouse is down at the bottom of the ivy-roots, asleep. The hedgehog is snoring in a hole in the bank over there. The frog is at the bottom of the pond, and the toad asleep under a stone. The lizard is in a hollow stump, and the snake sleeps with his brothers in an old tree. The little black bat is asleep too, hanging upside down in the barn."

"Asleep! Why are they all asleep?" said the hare.

"Well, they always sleep the winter away—didn't you know that?" said the rabbit scornfully. "It's no good having a party at this time of year. But cheer up—I and my family will come if you like. We shan't eat the tea you've got ready—but we'll all play games."

So they did, and the hare enjoyed himself after all. But none of his real guests came to the party—they wouldn't wake up till the spring-time.

The Clever Little Cat

JOHN and Shirley had a little cat. They had had him since he was a kitten, and they called him Zebby, because he was striped like a zebra.

Zebby was a clever little thing. He hadn't grown very big, but he was strong and healthy. He mewed with joy whenever he saw John and Shirley, for they loved him and were kind to him.

They taught Zebby quite a lot of tricks. The little cat could rattle the handle of a door by standing on his hind legs. He could play hide-and-seek with the children. He could sit up and beg just like a dog.

He rubbed himself aganist the children's legs, and purred when he sat on their knees.

"He sounds like the mowing-machine!" said Shirley, tickling

Zebby round the ears to make him purr more loudly.

But Mother wasn't quite so pleased with Zebby. "He's a little thief!" she said. "If the larder door is left open he creeps inside and takes whatever he can! And he makes such a noise at night, too, if he's left out. He won't come in when he's called—so he has to be left out—and then he yowls the place down!"

"Oh, Mother. Zebby's a darling!" said John, and picked up the purring little cat.

"Well, darling or not, Zebby will have to go to another home if he doesn't stop stealing!" said Mother.

"Do you hear that, Zebby?" asked Shirley. "You must stop at once, because we couldn't bear to lose you. Come and play ball with us."

Zebby ran across the grass with John and Shirley. He was very good with a ball. Whenever he found one he rolled it along with his paw, pretended it was a mouse, jumped at it, sidled all round it, and then set it rolling again. There was nothing he loved quite so much as a ball.

For two days Zebby was very good. Then Mother and Daddy were going to have a tennis-party, and Mother got in some salmon to make sandwiches— and, will you believe it, Zebby smelt out that salmon, watched till the larder door was open, and walked in! He hid under the shelf when he heard Cook coming, but as soon as she was out of the way,

Zebby jumped up on the shelf and began to eat that nice pink salmon!

So, when Cook went to fetch it for the sandwiches, there was no salmon to be seen, except a bone on the plate, licked quite bare!

"That cat again!" cried Cook, and went to tell Mother, who was changing into her tennis things. Mother was very angry.

"You'll have to open the potted meat, Cook," she said. "The bad little cat! I won't keep him in the house a week longer!"

She hunted for Zebby to give him a smacking, but the little cat had run away to hide. Zebby knew quite well he had done wrong, and he wanted to find somewhere safe.

He ran upstairs. He went into the loft. He jumped out of the loft window on to the roof, and found a nice warm place by the chimney. He curled himself up and went to sleep. Nobody would find him there!

Cook made some potted-meat sandwiches. Mother and Daddy went out to put up the net, and the children tipped out nine new balls on to the green lawn. The guests began to arrive.

John and Shirley were ball-boys. They hunted for the balls that ran into the bushes or bounced over the net into the long orchard grass. They talked about naughty little Zebby.

"I do wish Mother would let up keep Zebby,"

said Shirley. "He's been ours for three years now, and he's the nicest little cat I know."

"I wonder where he is," said John. "He's jolly clever at hiding himself when he's naughty!"

They soon knew where he was! One of the guests hit a ball very wildly and it went spinning up, up, up to the roof of the house! It fell right on Zebby, who was asleep by the chimney, and he woke with a loud squeak of fright. The ball dropped down the roof to the gutter and stayed there.

"There's Zebby!" said Shirley. "Up on the roof! That ball must have woken him up! Zebby, Zebby, Zebby! Come on down!"

But Zebby didn't. He lay there sleepily watching the tennis. Soon another ball flew up on the roof and stuck in the gutter. Zebby watched it with much interest. He got up and strolled down the sloping roof to the gutter.

Mother was sorry that the balls had gone there because nobody could get them, and they would go rotten in the next rainstorm. But Zebby began to play with the two balls, trying to get them out of the wet gutter.

One ball came out and dropped down to the ground with a big bounce. The children gave a shriek of delight. "Mother, Zebby's getting the roof-balls for you!"

Zebby scooped out the second one, but before he could play with it, it dropped to the ground, of course! Everybody laughed and cheered.

"Two good balls saved!" said Daddy. "Thank you, Zebby!"

Zebby waited up on the roof for more balls. Soon one came—and then another—for the court was really too near the house, and many a time balls had been lost in the gutters. Zebby waited for the balls, and wherever they happened to stick he ran to them, and pawed them until he got them free. Then down they fell to the ground.

"What a clever little cat!" cried all the guests. "You must be proud of him! How useful he will be at tennis-parties, too—you will never lose balls in the gutter again!"

Well, Mother and Daddy did begin to feel very proud of Zebby!

"He's saved no end of new balls for us today," said Daddy. "Can't we keep the larder door shut, Mother, and keep Zebby?"

"I really think we'd better try," said Mother—and how John and Shirley cheered! So a weight was fixed to the larder door, and whenever it was left open by mistake the door closed itself—so Zebby could never get inside to steal again.

He's still living with John and Shirley, and when I go there to play tennis I love to see him sitting on the roof waiting for the balls. Sometimes we send one up there just for fun—we do love to see him paw it out of the gutter and send it down to the ground once more! Isn't he clever?

Sneezing Powder

ONCE upon a time there lived a brownie called Smarty. He kept a little shop in Hallo Town, in which he sold jars of honey, fine yellow lemons, and big yellow pills that helped to cure colds.

In the winter-time Smarty did a fine trade, for anyone who had a cold came to buy his honey, his juicy lemons, and his cold-pills. Then they would go home, squeeze the lemons into a glass, put in hot water and sugar and a spoonful or two of Smarty's golden honey, take a cold-pill, and go to bed—and lo and behold, next morning they were cured!

But in the summer-time nobody seemed to have a cold at all. It was most annoying for Smarty. Instead of thinking of selling something else, such as ice-creams or cool lemon drinks, Smarty still went on hoping that people would have colds and buy his cold cure. So he wasn't quite as smart as his name, was he?

He was quite smart enough to think out a naughty trick, though!

"If only I could *make* people think they had a

cold, they would come and buy my honey and lemons and pills," thought Smarty. "If only they would sneeze or cough just as they passed my shop, it would be so easy for me to say, 'Dear me! You are getting a cold! Buy my cold-cure before you are very bad!' But nobody ever sneezes outside my shop."

Smarty sat and thought for a bit, and then he grinned all over his sly little face. He slapped his knee in delight. He had thought of a wonderful idea!

"I'll go and buy some sneezing powder from old Dame Flap!" he said to himself. "And I'll put some into my pepper-pot and shake it out of my bedroom window whenever anyone passes! Then they will sneeze hard, and perhaps come and buy my goods."

So off he went to buy the sneezing powder. He paid Dame Flap ten pence for a boxful and she wrapped it up for him. It was a queer powder, rather like a fine green flour, and it had a strange smell.

Smarty ran home with it. He emptied some into his pepper-pot and slipped upstairs to his bedroom window, which was just over his shop. He leaned out in excitement. Was anybody coming?

Yes—here was Old Man Shuffle! Smarty waited till he was underneath the window and then he shook out some of the powder. It went on Old Man Shuffle's nose, and he stopped. He took out his big blue handkerchief and held it to his nose.

"Whooosh!" he sneezed. "A-whooosh!"

"Hi, Old Man Shuffle, you've got a dreadful cold!" called Smarty. "Come into my shop and get some honey and lemons and pills!"

So in shuffled the old fellow, thinking it was very lucky that he should be outside Smarty's shop just when his cold had begun. He bought a jar of honey, two lemons, and a box of yellow pills. Smarty grinned. He ran up to his bedroom again.

"Ah! Here are Mr. Twiddle and his wife!" chuckled Smarty. He shook his pepper-pot over them. They stopped and fumbled for their hankies.

"Er-tish-oo!" said Mr. Twiddle loudly.

"Ish-ish-ish!" sneezed Mrs. Twiddle politely into her handkerchief.

"ER-TISH-OOO!" went Mr. Twiddle.

"Not so much noise, Twiddle," said Mrs.

Twiddle. "Ish-ish-ish-ish! Dear me! We are beginning colds, I think. Look, let's buy some honey and lemons, and maybe we'll stop our colds from getting bad."

So into Smarty's shop they went and bought what they wanted, much to Smarty's delight. As soon as they had gone, he popped upstairs again with his pepper-pot full of sneezing powder.

He made Twinkle the pixie sneeze and buy honey and pills. He made Mr. Meddle sneeze so strongly that his hat flew on to the roof and he had to get a ladder to fetch it. He made Dame Winks sneeze twelve times, and at the end her bonnet was right over her nose and she couldn't see where she was going at all.

Oh, Smarty had plenty of fun that day, and he made plenty of money, too! But when everyone found that they had no cold at all when they got home, and didn't need the honey and lemons, they were rather puzzled. They talked about it to one another, and they found that all of them had begun their sneezing fits outside Smarty's shop.

"Very nice for Smarty!" said Mr. Meddle. "Let us go along and see what we can see."

So they all went back towards Smarty's shop, and peeped round the corner. And they saw Smarty leaning out of his bedroom window, pepper-pot in hand!

"Aha!" said Old Man Shuffle angrily. "So that's his trick, is it! Come along, everybody!"

They all went into Smarty's shop. Smarty hurried down to serve them. Mrs. Twiddle was waiting for him. She snatched the pepper-pot out of his pocket and shook it all over Smarty.

"Colds are catching today!" she said. "Sneeze, Smarty, sneeze! Dear, dear! You must have caught our colds."

"Whoosh!" said Smarty. "Atish-oo! Ish-ish-ish! Osha-whoosh! Tish-oo!"

Mrs. Twiddle emptied all the sneezing powder over him. My goodness, Smarty simply could *not* stop sneezing! It was dreadful!

"By the time you've finished I guess you'll want to buy a pot of your own honey, a dozen lemons, and a box of pills!" said Mr. Twiddle, laughing. "Good-bye, Smarty. It serves you right!"

They all went out, giggling and chuckling, and they could hear Smarty's sneezes all the way down the road.

Poor Smarty! He sneezed all that day and all that night, and by that time his nose and throat and eyes were so sore that he had to take two jars of honey, six lemons, and a box of pills to cure himself!

Now he has shut up his shop and gone out selling ice-creams. And a very much better idea too, in the summer—don't you think so?

The Giant
Limber-Lumber

IN the Fairy Queen's dining-room there was one tall golden candle-stick on the mantelpiece. Once there had been two, but the other had been stolen.

"I do so wish I knew where the other was," said the Queen one day. "One looks so silly, standing there all alone."

"I have heard that the Giant Limber-Lumber has it," said the King, looking up from his newspaper. "It is said that his servant Peto was passing here one morning, and when he saw our candle-sticks, he hopped in by the window and took one. He gave it to Limber-Lumber, who has had it on his kitchen mantelpiece ever since."

"Well!" said the Queen, amazed. "Fancy that. I wonder you haven't sent to fetch it away, my dear."

"The Giant Limber-Lumber is rather too big to offend," said the King. "I don't think anyone would dare to ask him for the candle-stick."

Now it so happened that little Prince Gladsome was sitting on the floor looking at a book, and he heard what the King and Queen said.

"*I'll* go and get that candle-stick for you, Mother!" he cried, and before the Queen could stop him, he had kissed her and run out of the room.

He jumped on to his pony and galloped off before anyone knew what he was doing.

It was a long way to Limber-Lumber's castle, and by the time Gladsome arrived there it was night. He saw the great building rising up in the dark, and he made his way up the steps to the front door. He clattered on it with his riding whip, and soon it opened.

"Come in," said Peto, the giant's servant, and Gladsome stepped inside. He walked boldly into the great kitchen, and looked about for his mother's candle-stick. Giant Limber-Lumber was sitting down in an enormous chair, polishing the silver buttons on his coat. He was most surprised to see Gladsome.

"I've come for my mother's candle-stick," said Gladsome, pointing to where it glittered on the mantelpiece.

"Ho!" said the giant mockingly. "You have, have you? Well, you won't get it! And what's more, I've a good mind to fatten you up and have you for my next Sunday dinner."

"I shouldn't let you do that," said Gladsome boldly, though his heart beat very fast with fear. "You don't know how strong I am! You be careful I don't knock you down."

"Ho, ho, ha ha!" roared the giant, laughing very loudly indeed. "Whoever heard of such a thing! You tiny little mannikin, I could bowl you over with my little finger. But wait! If you really think you are stronger than I am, I will give you a chance to prove it."

"I am quite willing," said Gladsome.

"If you prove yourself stronger than I am, you shall have the candle-stick," said the giant. "But if I am stronger you shall be my Sunday dinner. It is too dark now to do anything, but tomorrow morning we will try!"

"I will get a bed ready for the Prince," said Peto, and he put a mattress on the floor, with a couple of blankets. They were very enormous, and the Prince felt quite lost when he cuddled down in them. Soon he was asleep, and did not wake until the sun streamed into the kitchen window.

He heard the giant talking to his servant Peto.

"I shall try him with two things," said Limber-Lumber. "First we will see who can squeeze the most juice out of a stone, and then we will see who can throw the stone the farthest."

When he heard that, Gladsome slipped out of bed and ran outside. He went to an orange tree and picked a small green orange, which he put in his pocket. Then he called a little sparrow to him.

"Sit in my warm pocket for a little while," he begged, and the sparrow hopped into his hand and allowed the Prince to put it carefully into his pocket.

Just then Limber-Lumber came outside, and called Gladsome.

"Breakfast!" he shouted in his thunderous voice. "Then for our trials of strength!"

Gladsome ate a large breakfast, and so did the giant. Then out they went into the fields.

"Now first," said the giant with a grin, "we will each try to squeeze juice from a stone. I'll try first."

He picked up a large stone and began to squeeze it between his enormous hands. So great was his strength that tiny drops of water came from it and dripped to the ground.

"There!" said the giant, pleased. "Now you try."

Gladsome pretended to pick up a stone, but as he bent down he took the little orange from his pocket. He stood up with it between his hands. Then he squeezed it.

Out came a stream of yellow drops, and Limber-Lumber shouted in surprise and rage.

"It's quite easy," said Gladsome. "I am astonished you could only get a few drops of water from your stone."

The giant growled angrily, and picked up another stone, a smooth round one.

"Now I will throw this into the air," he said, "and you will see how very far it goes. Then you shall try."

He threw it into the air and Gladsome marvelled to see it go so high and so far. It fell quite a mile away.

"Now you try," said Limber-Lumber, and Gladsome once more bent down, pretending to pick up a stone. But as he stooped he took the little sparrow from his pocket and held it closely in his hand.

Then he threw it high into the air and once it had gained its balance it flew off. On it went, getting smaller and smaller and smaller, until at last it was quite out of sight.

"Your stone has gone so far that I can't see where it will fall," said the giant, looking at Gladsome in wonder. "You must indeed be strong."

"Yes," said the little Prince. "If you dared to try to eat me for your Sunday dinner, I should take hold of you by your hair and throw you into the sea, which is quite five miles away. So be careful. Now let us go back to your castle, and get the candle-stick."

They went back, and Limber-Lumber lifted down the golden candle-stick.

"Carry it to my pony," said the Prince, feeling sure that it would be too heavy for him to take. So the giant obediently carried the candle-stick to his pony and placed it on his back.

"Good-bye," said Gladsome, jumping up behind the candle-stick. "And don't you dare to steal anything again!"

He raised his horse-whip, and the giant fell back in fear, thinking that Gladsome really could whip him. He tumbled over Peto his servant, and they both rolled on the ground. Off rode the Prince, laughing to see such a funny sight.

When he arrived at his own palace, the King and Queen rushed to meet him, and *weren't* they surprised to see the candle-stick?

The Robber Who Wasn't There

IT was a lovely spring day, and the sun shone down warmly. The primroses began to open in the garden, and George and Nora went to pick a bunch for the nursery table.

Happy, their dog, went with them. He ran round the garden, smelling here and there, just as happy as his name. He ran to the wood-shed and smelt the soot-water there that the gardener had prepared for watering later on.

And when he got to the wood-shed, he cocked up his ears and then began to bark madly! How he barked!

"Woof, woof, woof! Woof, woof, woof!"

"Whatever's the matter, Happy?" cried Nora, in surprise. "You'll bark your head off soon, and then what will you do?"

"Woof, woof, woof!" barked Happy, and he scraped at the shed door with his paw.

"He wants to go in," said George. "I wonder why?"

Happy stopped barking and stood listening to

something inside the shed, his head well on one side. The children listened too.

There was a noise inside the shed! It was a funny noise—a kind of scrapy, scrambly noise—and then a pot fell over and broke!

The children jumped and looked scared.

"Woof, woof, woof!" barked Happy again, and he scraped at the wooden door as if he would like to break it down.

"There's somebody hiding in there," said Nora.

"Who could it be?" said George, in a frightened whisper.

"A robber!" whispered back Nora. "Oh dear, George, I feel frightened. Let's go and tell Mother."

They waited for a moment, and then they heard the noise inside the shed again. Another pot fell over, and the children jumped and ran away. Happy stayed behind, barking, and pawing at the door.

"There's one thing—the robber won't escape from the shed whilst Happy is barking outside," panted George, as the two children ran to the house.

"No—so he's a prisoner till we get somebody to catch him!" said Nora.

They rushed into the house and called for Mother. "Mother! Mother! Come quickly! Where are you?"

But Mother was out. So they ran to tell Jane the housemaid. "Jane! Jane! There's a robber in the wood-shed!" said George. "Will you come and catch him?"

"Good gracious, no!" cried Jane, quite alarmed. "I'm not going robber-catching! I'll tell Cook!"

So Jane, George and Nora ran to the kitchen to tell the cook about the robber in the wood-shed. Cook was surprised to see them all running at top speed into her kitchen.

"What's the matter?" she said. "Is the cat chasing you?"

"Oh, Cook, there's a robber in the wood-shed!" panted Jane. "Get your rolling-pin and come and catch him."

"Indeed, I won't," said Cook at once. "A robber should be caught by the policeman. He'll be by here directly. We'll watch for him and tell him. Fancy that now—a robber in the wood-shed!"

"Happy is keeping him prisoner till we get somebody to catch the robber," said Nora, feeling tremendously excited. "Can't you hear him barking like mad?"

They could. "Woof, woof, woof!"

"Here comes the policeman!" said Cook at last, and they saw the big burly policeman walking slowly down their road. George, Nora, Jane, and Cook all flew out to the front gate and called to him.

"Hi! Policeman! We've got a robber here!"

"What did you say?" asked the policeman in great surprise, and he took out his notebook and pencil.

"Oh, there's no time to be writing notes," cried

Jane the housemaid. "There's a robber in the wood-shed and the dog's guarding him. He'll be a very fierce robber, and maybe he'll fight you, Policeman. Hadn't you better get someone to help you?"

"Oh no," said the policeman, rather grandly. "I'm quite used to robbers."

So George, Nora, Jane, Cook, and the policeman all went down the garden to the wood-shed, where Happy was still barking.

"Now just listen, everyone!" said George.

So they all listened, and sure enough they could hear the noise in the wood-shed all right—and two more pots fell over with a crash! Even the policeman jumped, and as for Jane, she ran half-way up the garden in fright.

"Now here's a strange thing," said the policeman, suddenly pointing to the door. "It's locked on the outside, for there's the key in the lock, and it's turned! Now how did the robber get in there, and yet lock the door on the outside?"

Everybody stared at the lock, but nobody could think how a robber could lock himself in and yet leave the key outside. It was a mystery.

The policeman unlocked the door and shouted out in a loud, stern voice, "Come out, there! Come out at once!"

Everyone waited to see who would come out— but nobody did! Another plant-pot fell over. The policeman grew angry.

"Am I to go in after you? Come out at once!" But

still nobody came out. So the policeman bravely stuck his head inside the dark shed and looked around.

"There's nobody here!" he said in the greatest astonishment. "Well—that's queer!"

Everybody looked inside—and sure enough there was no robber there at all. Happy darted round and round the shed, sniffling happily. Everyone went out again and talked hard.

"Then who made that noise?"

"There *was* somebody there!"

"And it must have been a robber!"

"How could he have got away?"

And suddenly they heard the noise again! They all stared at the door, feeling quite scared.

Then the robber walked out! Yes—he really did! And who do you suppose it was? Why, nobody else but Crawler, the old tortoise, who had been put there asleep in a box for the winter! He had wakened up, scrambled out of his box, and crawled round the shed, knocking over pots as he went. Well, well, well!

He walked out into the warm spring sunshine, and blinked his eyes at everyone. Happy danced round him, barking. Everyone went red and looked foolish.

Then George laughed—and Nora joined in. Jane giggled and Cook roared. The policeman opened his big mouth and ha-ha-ha'd too. It was surprising to hear them, and Crawler the tortoise was frightened. He hissed and popped his head under his shell!

"The robber who wasn't there!" cried Nora, pointing to the tortoise. "Oh, Crawler, what a fright you gave us!"

Poor Mister Booh

MISTER BOOH was a fat little man who lived in Chubby Cottages, down Lemon Lane. He was fat because he lived on lots of butter, eggs, cream, and milk, and he liked being fat. He said it made him feel good-tempered.

Now one day he went to a meeting to decide whether or not Lemon Lane should be widened. There was a very narrow place in the middle of it and carts couldn't pass each other there, but were always getting stuck. So Mister Booh and all the other folk living in Lemon Lane went to talk about it and to see what should be done.

Mister Booh put on his new rubber boots, because it was raining. He took his brown gloves, too, because his hands got cold very easily. Then he went off to the meeting.

Everybody talked a great deal and they all enjoyed themselves very much and felt very grand. Nothing was decided, but they said they would meet again the very next week and have another talk. Then they all went out into the hall to put on their outdoor things to go home.

Mister Booh put on his rubber boots, and took his brown gloves from the hall-stand. Then he said good-bye to everyone and started off for home.

He put on his gloves as he went, and they somehow seemed rather big. His boots flip-flapped as he went too, and this surprised Mister Booh very much. He looked down at them and saw that they really hardly fitted his feet.

"Well, that's funny," he said. "Have my feet gone smaller? They fitted me well enough when I bought them last week."

Then he looked at his gloves and was more surprised than ever.

"They seemed too big too," he said. "Oh dear, I'm getting thin! I wonder why that is? I must be ill. Yes, that's it, I'm going to be ill, and that's why my hands and feet are thinner and my shoes and gloves too big."

He was very much worried, and decided to call at the doctor's and tell him. So when he came to Doctor Come-in's brass plate, he went in and knocked at the door.

Doctor Come-in was at home.

"What's the matter with you?" he asked Mister Booh. "You look worried."

"Yes, Doctor, and I *feel* worried," said poor Mister Booh. "I've got much thinner in a week."

"Dear me, you look as fat as ever to me," said Doctor Come-in.

"Well, I'm not," said Mister Booh, and he showed the doctor how very much too big his boots and his gloves were. "That will show you how much thinner I've got in a week, because when I bought these new last week they fitted me very well indeed."

"Dear, dear, you must be wasting away," said Doctor Come-in. "Well, never mind—we'll soon put you right. You must eat plenty of cream, butter, and eggs, and drink lots of milk. Then you'll soon be as fat as ever again."

"Well, I eat all those now," said Mister Booh.

"Eat twice as much then," said the doctor, " and come and see me again in a week's time."

Mister Booh went home, still very much worried. He ordered twice as many eggs and twice as much butter, cream, and milk as usual. His milkman was so pleased. Mister Booh stayed indoors all that week, because he wanted to give himself a chance to get fat again.

And do you know, when the day came for him to go to the next meeting about the widening of the narrow place in Lemon Lane, he could only just get his rubber boots on! And he split the gloves—so that shows you how much bigger his hands had grown!

He was delighted. He walked to the meeting, took off his rubber boots and gloves, and went into the dining-room, where everybody was talking nineteen to the dozen.

After the meeting was over, and still nothing was decided at all, they went out into the hall again to get their things. Mister Booh found his boots, but dear, dear me, what was his surprise to find that he couldn't *possibly* get them on! They were about two sizes too small. And as for his gloves, well, he couldn't even get his thumb into the thumb-hole!

"But I can't have grown so much fatter just in the meeting," he cried, quite frightened. Everybody crowded round him to see what was the matter, and he told them.

"Oh, please," said a small voice, "I think I can explain."

Mister Booh turned round and saw a very tall, thin man with large feet and hands. He was wearing rubber boots and gloves that had split down the side.

"Well, explain then," said Mister Booh.

"You see, last week someone went off with my new rubber boots," said the tall man in a meek voice, "and my gloves too. He left me his small boots and gloves instead, and I had a dreadful time getting home in the boots. I didn't know whose they were, but I thought perhaps they would be brought back to this meeting, and they were. I've got them on now. Those that you have now are *really* yours, Mister Booh, and I can't think why you can't get them on."

"But I know why," groaned poor Mister Booh. "Oh dear, oh dear. I didn't guess I had on gloves and boots belonging to a bigger person than me. I thought they were my own, and I was very much worried because I felt sure my feet and hands had gone thin. So I went to the doctor and he told me how to get fatter—and now that I have my own boots and gloves back again I'm too fat to get them on."

"Poor Mister Booh," said everyone. "Whatever will you do?"

Well, of course he couldn't do anything except walk home in his stockinged feet and carry his gloves instead of wearing them. And he was very much afraid that he wouldn't be able to wear his other shoes either, or any of his gloves, and even his new suit was too tight for him.

He went past the doctor's house very quickly, because he knew that Doctor Come-in would be expecting him that day, and he didn't want to go in and explain that he really hadn't been getting thinner after all, and was now much too fat. No, the doctor would laugh if he knew that.

So he went sadly home, making no noise at all in his stockinged feet, wishing and wishing that he hadn't eaten so much butter, cream, and eggs, and thinking of all the new clothes he would have to buy.

Poor Mister Booh!